c.1 $20.—

YOUTH SERVICES

SPORTS FROM COAST TO COAST™

FOOTBALL

RULES, TIPS, STRATEGY, AND SAFETY

— BRIAN WINGATE —

rosen publishing's
rosen
central®

New York

To Cora, a growing football fan

Published in 2007 by The Rosen Publishing Group, Inc.
29 East 21st Street, New York, NY 10010

Copyright © 2007 by The Rosen Publishing Group, Inc.

First Edition

Library of Congress Cataloging-in-Publication Data

Wingate, Brian.
Football: rules, tips, strategy, and safety/Brian Wingate.
   p. cm.—(Sports from coast to coast)
Includes bibliographical references and index.
ISBN-13: 978-1-4042-0993-0
ISBN-10: 1-4042-0993-X (library binding)
1. Football—Miscellanea—Juvenile literature. I. Title. II. Series.
GV950.7.W56 2006
796.332—dc22

                                                    2006009202

Printed in China

CONTENTS

CHAPTER ONE

A Great Accident: The Birth of American Football

A young player leaps past a defender in this 1894 illustration of an American football game. Players back then wore shin guards, but they did not wear helmets or shoulder pads.

Like many great inventions, American football came about by a series of fortunate accidents. Legend says that in 1823, a group of English lads were playing English football on their school grounds. The sport was a lot like soccer in that most players were not allowed to use their hands. The players who could use their hands were not allowed to run more than a few yards while holding the ball.

On this particular day, the bell tower was about to strike five o'clock. According to school rules, the game would end with the last toll of the bell. As the bell began to chime, a young man named William Webb Ellis caught a long pass. After catching the ball, he was supposed to place it on the ground for a free kick. Instead, he held the ball and dashed across the goal line for the winning score. His teammates thought this new twist on the rules made for a more exciting game. Eventually, the idea of running with the ball took root, and the sport of English football began to change. Players who liked this different approach formed a new sport—rugby.

Early Rugby in the United States

Rugby-style football grew in popularity and soon crossed the Atlantic Ocean. By the 1840s, young men were playing the sport at colleges throughout the northeastern United States. On November 6, 1869, Princeton University and Rutgers University played the first football game between two college teams. With more than two hundred spectators watching the action, it was clear that the sport had the potential to attract fans. Teams did not always play by the same rules, however, so it was sometimes difficult to arrange matches. For this first game, the captains from each team agreed to follow the official rules of the London Football Association, which were familiar to most players.

This first intercollegiate football game still looked more like soccer than the football we know today. The field was large but crowded, with twenty-five men playing at a time on each side. The idea was to advance a round, soccer-type ball over the opponent's goal line. As a player moved the ball toward the goal line, his teammates formed a wall in front of him, blocking and barreling through opposing players.

Players moved the ball by kicking or batting it with their hands, feet, heads, and sides; they were not allowed to throw it. Players were allowed to catch the ball, but they could not run with it. When a player's progress was stopped, he was required to place the ball on the ground and kick it away.

Students at Columbia University practice football in this photo from about 1908. Note that by this time, some players preferred to protect their heads with leather helmets.

As the sport grew in popularity, teams continued to experiment with the rules, trying to find just the right balance.

Football Rules Take Shape

In 1874, a rugby team from Canada added some new flavors to the mix. Players from McGill University, in Montreal, challenged the football team from Harvard, in Boston, to several games. The Canadian players used an egg-shaped ball that bounced unpredictably. They awarded a team a "touch-down" when the ball carrier crossed the opponent's goal line. In addition, the Canadian rugby players could kick "field goals" with precision. The Harvard players loved these differences, and they quickly imported them into the American game.

A couple years later, in 1876, 2,000 fans paid to watch Yale University and Harvard play this new brand of football. One year later, the Intercollegiate Football Association was created, and the American style of football was officially born.

Seeing the Future

One young man, Walter Camp, fell in love with football when he watched Yale and Harvard clash in 1876. Camp attended Yale himself and was the captain of the football team from 1878 to 1881. During his career, he came up with many rule changes that he thought would improve the game for players and spectators alike. In 1880, the International Football Association (IFA) started to use some of Camp's ideas. For his many contributions to the game, Walter Camp is now known as the father of college football.

Camp thought that fifty people on the field at one time created too much chaos, so he suggested eleven players per team. Then the field size could be reduced, making the game

Walter Camp (*above*) helped transform the sport of rugby into American football. As a player, coach, author, and sports committee member, Camp was active in the sport for more than fifty years.

A Passing Fancy

Today's game looks a lot different from the game Walter Camp played. Football started mostly as a running game, and the sport's first stars were runners and blockers. In fact, prior to 1906, forward passes were against the rules.

Most players didn't want to throw the ball anyway. Early footballs were large and rounded on the ends, like a watermelon. In addition, they leaked air constantly. It was much safer to run with the ball than throw a floppy, deflating melon. The forward pass became popular, though, because it opened up the field for more exciting play.

In 1912, college football reduced the size of the ball to make it easier to throw. Manufacturing also improved, and by 1924, Wilson Sporting Goods Co. had developed a double-lined ball that reduced air leakage. Soon, quarterbacks were throwing long passes with precision, and burly running backs had to share the spotlight with the more graceful quarterbacks. Today, the quarterback is usually the most recognizable player on the field.

easier to watch from the sidelines. Camp's most revolutionary idea was creating the line of scrimmage. Before this was invented, each play started with the ball thrown by an official into the middle of a large group. All the players pushed and jostled and tried to kick the ball out to a teammate. This player could then try to break free and score. It was an exciting style of play, but the drawback was that each game was ninety minutes of crazed running, tackling, and fighting for the ball. Camp thought that if a player was tackled, or downed, his team should get more chances to advance the ball. With a line of scrimmage as a starting point, a team would get a certain number of "downs" to advance the ball at least five yards. The line of scrimmage allowed teams to run more set plays and use special strategies.

Football Goes Pro

As more and more fans came out to watch college games, it became clear that football could also be a profitable business. Athletic clubs across Pennsylvania began fielding their own teams. The clubs' communities paid to watch the games and support the teams. Then, in 1892, the Allegheny (Pennsylvania) Athletic Association paid a $500 "performance bonus" to Pudge Heffelfinger, making him the first professional American football player.

Before long, professional teams sprouted up all over the Northeast. In 1920, the American Professional Football Association (APFA) was formed with a total of ten teams. Typically, team owners were businesspeople who saw their teams as good advertising opportunities. Every team lost money the first year, but the league managed to survive and grow. In 1922, the APFA changed its name to the National Football League (NFL). Teams continued to attract more and more spectators, and according to a recent ESPN poll, the NFL is now the most popular sports league in the United States. The championship of the NFL—the Super Bowl—has become a worldwide event. Millions of people around the globe watch two teams compete for the Super Bowl title every year.

The NFL is not the only show in town. Thousands of fans in Canada enjoy the action of the Canadian Football League (CFL) or cheer their favorite stars on the indoor turf of the Arena Football League. Of course, college football is still a grand tradition. And every summer and fall, kids across North America suit up to start a new youth league football season.

CHAPTER TWO

The Players

From far above, a football field looks like a giant game board, with the players being the game pieces. A football game tests players' physical skill, strength, speed, and athletic ability. It is also very much a mental game, as teams try to outwit each other in a clash of strategies. Each individual member plays a special role in the bigger scheme of the team game.

It can seem confusing at first to see twenty-two players burst into action all at once. But as you learn the positions and roles for each player on the field, you'll see that the game is not that hard to understand. Watch enough football, and you'll probably want to get on the field and give it a try.

If you have never played football before, descriptions of the player positions in this chapter may help you figure out which one would be good for you.

The offensive linemen crouch as the quarterback calls out a play. Once they are set, the linemen must not move from their stance until the center hikes the ball.

Putting the Team Together

There are three main groupings of players on a football team: offense, defense, and special teams. Individual players may play on one, two, or even all three of these units. But only one set of players from each team is on the field at a time.

Offense

To win a football game, a team has to score points. That's the job of the offense. They move the ball down the field and try to score a touchdown or kick a field goal. The offense has eleven players on the field at a time, all working together to move the ball forward.

Quarterback

The quarterback (QB) is the leader of the offense. This player guides the team down the field, usually handling the football on every play. Before each play, the offensive players get together in a huddle, and the quarterback calls out which play to run. A good QB is calm under pressure and understands the flow of the game. As a play unfolds, the QB makes a handoff to a running back or throws a pass to a receiver. Quarterbacks are usually good overall athletes. They must be tall enough to see over the players in front of them and strong enough to throw the ball quickly and accurately.

Quarterback Tip: Throwing a Perfect Spiral

- Hold the ball with your ring finger just in front of the last lace on the football. Leave an empty space, and place your little finger between the next two laces.
- Raise your nonthrowing hand and let it swing out away from your body as you twist at the waist to throw. Keep the elbow up on your throwing arm.
- Squeeze the ball just before you throw it, and then flick your wrist downward as you let go and follow through.

Your whole body is used to make a perfect pass. A balanced stance provides stability. Power comes from twisting your hips and shoulders. Finesse and a good touch come from your arm and hand.

Offensive Line Tip: Setting Up in a Good Stance

- Keep your feet no farther apart than the width of your shoulders.
- Point your toes straight ahead.
- Once your feet are set, drop into a squatting position and extend your down hand slightly inside your near foot, forming a tripod. Use the hand closer to the ball as your down hand.
- Keep your shoulders square to the line of scrimmage and parallel to the ground. Keep your back flat, with your shoulders elevated slightly.
- Keep your head up.

Offensive Backfield and Wide Receivers

Lining up behind the quarterback, the running back and the fullback handle most of the running plays in football. When the running back gets the ball, the fullback charges ahead of him, blocking players from the other team.

Wide receivers usually line up at the line of scrimmage, out near the sidelines. When the ball is snapped, the wide receivers streak down the field to catch a pass from the quarterback. Receivers run a specific pattern on the field for each play so the QB knows where to throw the ball. On a running play, there is no pass to catch, so the receiver blocks opponents for the runner.

Wide receivers work closely with quarterbacks to time their routes on the field. This receiver won't have to break his stride as he catches the pass coming in over his shoulder.

Wide Receiver Tips: Catch and Run

- Catch the ball with your hands first, and then immediately bring the ball to rest against your body.
- Be sure you control the ball before you start running after the catch. It's easy to drop a pass if you're thinking too far ahead.

The quarterback looks to pass as his offensive line blocks the rush of defensive players. If the quarterback is provided with good protection, he has more time to find an open receiver downfield.

Offensive Line

The players on the offensive line block the charge of the defense and create a pocket of protection around the quarterback. In the middle of the offensive line is the center, who lines up in front of the quarterback. Before each play begins, a referee places the football on the ground. The center crouches down and places one hand on the ball. The quarterback shouts a series of numbers and words related to the play before calling "hike!" The center then snaps the ball back between his legs and jumps up to block the defense.

On either side of the center are the offensive guards. They "guard" the quarterback by blocking opponents with their arms and bodies. The offensive tackles line up outside the guards. The players on the offensive line are some of the strongest on the field. They must have a combination of strength and quickness to protect the quarterback.

Sometimes a tight end will line up next to a tackle on the end of the offensive line. Depending on the play, the tight end can block players from the other team or run out into the open field to catch a pass.

Defense

On the other side of the ball is the defense. The job of the defense is to shut down the offense from the other team and return the ball to their own offense. All good defensive players chase the play to its conclusion. At the whistle ending a play, all eleven defenders should either be at the tackle or on their way to it.

Defensive Line

Defensive linemen learn to react to the movement of the center's hand as he snaps the ball to the quarterback to start a play. The nose tackle (or nose guard) lines up directly across from the center. At the snap, the nose tackle rushes forward and tries to push the center back toward the quarterback, collapsing the pocket of protection. If a running

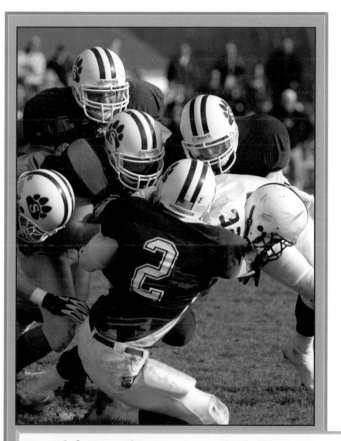

Five defensive players swarm the ball carrier (white jersey) and bring him to the ground. Gifted runners can evade single tacklers in the open field, but few can escape five tacklers at once.

Defensive Tip: Textbook Tackle

As you approach the ball carrier, stay low. Keep your weight forward, your back flat, and your knees bent. Like the tackler shown at right, you want to have your face mask at the near shoulder of the offensive player upon contact. Initiate the tackle with your shoulders and chest area first, rather than with your arms and hands. Once your

shoulders and chest make contact, wrap your arms around the ball carrier. Drive through the tackle, bringing your opponent to the ground.

back tries to run through the middle, the nose tackle tries to bring him to the ground.

Defensive tackles line up on either side of the nose tackle to stop the inside running game. They may also rush forward to pressure the quarterback. The defensive ends round out the defensive line. They stop runs to the outside and sometimes rush in from the sides to tackle the opposing quarterback.

Play continues until a ball carrier's knee hits the ground and the referee blows the whistle. Until the whistle sounds, defensive players—like those shown on the facing page—may pull and hack at the ball in an effort to force a fumble.

Defensive Backfield

The second line of defense is in the defensive backfield. These players patrol downfield and tackle any offensive ball carriers who advance beyond the line of scrimmage.

Linebackers stand behind the defensive line. They act as a lookout for the defense, trying to guess what play the offense is going to run. Good linebackers combine speed, size, and power. They sometimes face off against a big, strong offensive lineman, but they also may have to chase down a fleet wide receiver or running back.

Cornerbacks defend against the wide receivers. When the quarterback throws a pass, the cornerback's job is to knock it down or catch it himself. (When a defensive player catches the ball, it is called an interception.)

Safeties lurk in the deep part of the field and try to help out on every play. They rush in to break up passes and tackle ball carriers who have broken through the defensive front line.

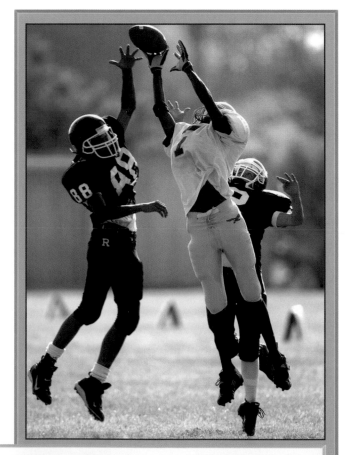

Teams often place two defenders on the opponent's best receiver. Above, a cornerback *(in dark jersey)* covers the receiver *(in light jersey)*, while a safety lurks behind the play.

Special Teams

Many games are won or lost through the play of special teams. These players take the field when the play involves a kick. On the kicking team, punters excel at booting the ball high and far down the field. Field

This kicker displays good form as he kicks off. With his supporting leg planted firmly beside the ball and arms out for stability, his right leg swings through the ball to send it downfield.

goal kickers, or placekickers, attempt to send the football sailing through the goalposts at the end of the field.

On the kick-receiving team, kick returners specialize in catching kickoffs and punts and running them back up the field while avoiding tacklers.

Coaching

With so many players on a football team, someone has to be the boss. This person is the head coach. Every team has a playbook, or collection of plays,

for offense, defense, and special teams. The head coach is usually the one who decides which play to run. A good head coach is very organized. In addition, coaches must be able to analyze the strategy of their opponents and adjust their own game plan during the course of play.

Youth league teams usually have one head coach and an assistant coach or two. (Professional teams have coaches for each position on the field.) Offensive and defensive coordinators are special assistant coaches who think up new strategies to win games.

A coach gives his quarterback a few pointers during a break in the game *(facing page)*. Good coaches use a variety of tactics to motivate their players to perform to the best of their abilities.

CHAPTER THREE

Playing the Game

In addition to the standard equipment, some players wear gloves to protect their hands or to get a better grip on a wet ball. This player also has a shield on his face mask to protect his eyes from debris or an accidental finger poke.

Before taking the field, players must be sure they are wearing proper protective gear. A football player getting dressed for a game is rather like a knight putting on a suit of armor before battle. Several layers of protection are required.

Equipment: Pads, Guards, and a Uniform

Football equipment is designed to protect your body from the impact of a strong tackle or a hard fall. In the locker room, players place padding over most areas of the body that hit the turf. Shoulder pads, hip pads, tail pads, and knee pads help cushion most falls. Thigh pads protect your legs from bruises. Some youth leagues require rib pads for added protection.

Once your pads are in place, you can pull on your pants and jersey. Your jersey has a number on it and colors that identify your team. For shoes, most leagues require players to wear rubber cleats. Your helmet is lined with protective padding, and a chin strap keeps it snug on your head. A molded plastic mouth guard protects your teeth. Once you're suited up, it's time to hit the field.

Let the Game Begin

Game action begins with the kickoff. A few members of both teams meet in the center of the field, and an official flips a coin to decide who will receive the ball first. Then the football is set on a one-inch plastic tee, and the players on the kicking team line up across the field. The placekicker boots the ball high into the air to a waiting member of the other team. The kickoff returner tries to run the ball back toward the end zone, dodging tackles. Usually, the kick returner either is tackled by the defense or steps out of bounds. The offense then comes onto the field to try to finish the drive.

Bring in the Offense: Four Downs

Let's say you are the quarterback. Your kick returner caught the kickoff and was forced out of bounds at your own thirty-yard line. You take the field with the rest of your offensive team. You have a set of four chances, or downs, to either score some points or gain ten yards. If you gain ten yards, you get another set of four downs to advance the ball.

On each play, you have three basic choices. You can hand the ball off to another player for a run play, you can throw the ball to a teammate down the

Dimensions of the Field

Every football field is a big rectangle. In the NFL and the NCAA (which governs American college football), the field is 120 yards long, including the end zones. It is 53⅓ yards wide. The middle of the field is lined with yard markers called hash marks. The lines marking every fifth yard run all the way across the field. The yards in between are marked with a small dash on the sidelines. This makes it easy for everyone to keep track of where plays start and end.

field for a pass play, or you can keep the ball and run with it yourself. The goal is always to get those ten yards or score some points.

First Down

You call your play in the huddle and then step up to the line of scrimmage. "Twenty-two . . . thirty-seven red . . . hike!" Your first play is a running play to the left side. Your offensive linemen block the defenders on the left side to create an opening for the runner. You hand your running back the ball, and a defensive tackle brings him down after a gain of two yards.

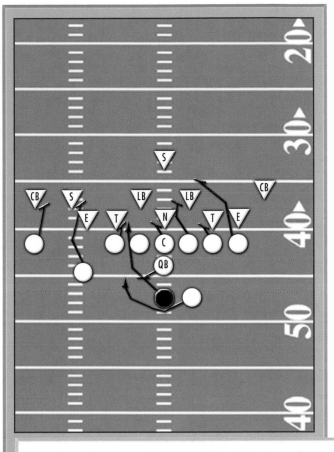

Coaches draw up diagrams like this to make plays easier to understand. Each player can see his task for the play and how it fits in with the movement of his teammates.

Second Down

It's second down, and you need eight yards to gain another first down. (So it's "second and eight.") You call a pass play. When the ball is snapped, you toss a pass to your tight end, but a defensive lineman reaches up and knocks the ball out of the air. It falls to the ground as an incomplete pass. The play is dead, and the ball will be placed back where it was before the down was played.

Third Down

It's now third and eight. You call another pass play. At the snap, one of your wide receivers runs forward several yards, and you loft a perfect pass into his arms. But as he catches the ball, a cornerback wraps him up and takes him down after a four-yard gain.

Fourth Down

After three plays, you have moved the ball six yards down the field. It's fourth and four—decision time. You could try a play to gain the ground you need. But if you don't make it, you must go to the sidelines and turn the ball over to the other team's offense. You are too far away to try for a field goal, so it's a good idea to punt the ball away. You want to pin the other team deep in its own territory, making it as hard as possible for them to reach your end zone.

Time to Punt

For a punt, the quarterback comes off the field, and a special kicker (the punter) comes into the game. The center hikes the ball back about ten yards to the punter, who catches it and kicks it down the field. The other team has a player waiting to receive the punt. He wants to catch the ball and race back to your end zone for a touchdown, but your special teams players will try to tackle him. The spot where he goes down or steps out of bounds is where the other team's offense will start with the ball.

The down box shows the down being played (in this case, fourth down). The tall orange measuring chain, to the right, is connected to another one by a chain exactly ten yards long. It is used to mark the distance to a first down.

Putting Points on the Board

In football, there are several ways to score. At each end of the field is an area ten yards deep called the end zone. The goal is to advance the ball into your opponent's end zone. This results in a touchdown worth six points.

After a touchdown, the placekicker can try to boot the ball through the goalposts for one additional point. Or a team may try a two-point conversion instead. They get one chance from several yards out to drive the ball into the end zone again. Most kickers easily make the short kick, so it is the safer option. Teams go for the two-point conversion only in special circumstances.

For a field goal try, the holder receives a long snap from the center and places the ball on its end for the kicker to send it sailing toward the goalposts.

Sometimes a team's offense nears the end zone but can't score a touchdown. If this happens, the placekicker comes on to try to kick a field goal through the goalposts at the back of the end zone. A field goal counts for three points. In the NFL, the goalposts are 18 feet 6 inches (5.6 meters) wide; NCAA and youth league posts are 23 feet 4 inches (7.1 m) wide.

The only other way to score is on a safety. This rare play occurs when the defense tackles a ball carrier in his own end zone, or if an offensive player fumbles the ball out of bounds through his own end zone. A safety counts as two points.

Sometimes the player waiting for the punt does not catch the ball. He may wave his arms in the air as the ball comes down, signaling a "fair catch." This means that no one may touch him and the offense will start at the spot where he catches the ball. The receiving player may also choose to step aside and let the punt hit the ground. As the ball bounces, any member of the kicking team may rush in and touch it (known as "downing" the ball). The receiving team will then start their offensive drive from that spot. If the ball touches a player on the receiving team, the ball is live, and either team can recover it.

If the ball is punted out of bounds crossing a sideline, the other team starts their new drive where the ball left the field of play. If the punt goes into the end zone, the other team starts their drive on their own twenty-yard line.

Sometimes the punting team will try to surprise the receiving team by faking a punt. For this trick fourth-down play, the kicking team comes on the field as if they are executing a standard punt play. As usual, the punter lines up ten yards behind the center and catches the long snap. But, instead of kicking the ball downfield, the punter runs with the ball to try to make a first down. Or, instead of running with the ball, the punter may pass it to a teammate running downfield. The fake punt is a risky play, but when it works, it can change the momentum of a game.

Game-Time Strategy

The basic strategy of football is simple: score points and stop your opponent from scoring. But football strategy can be very complex. Even the smallest decision can make a big difference in a tight game.

Sometimes a coach will try to slow down the pace of a game to keep the ball away from the other team. Running plays take more time off the game clock than do passing plays. So if a runner is gaining good yardage, the offense can grind out first downs and advance toward the goal line while the game clock ticks down. This means the opposing team will not have as much time to score when they get the ball back.

Some teams try to pass a lot at the beginning of the game to build a lead and then run the ball in the second half to protect the lead. Other teams will

This team faced an easy decision on fourth down. Pinned deep in their own territory, they had to punt the ball away to try to move their opponent farther from the end zone.

pass again and again, simply trying to score as many points as possible as quickly as possible. Good coaches are smart game managers who use all of the available resources to win.

Football Officials

Every football game is run by a team of officials on the field. They spread out and make sure that all the rules are being followed. It's not an easy job, as there is a lot of action happening quickly on every play, and there are

hundreds of rules that govern the game. NFL and college football teams use seven officials for every game. Other leagues use as few as two or three per game.

The referee is the official with the most authority. He wears a white hat, while the others wear black ones. In addition to the referee, other officials on the field may include the umpire and the head linesman, as well as the line judge, field judge, back judge, and side judge.

When an official spots a violation of the rules, he may blow his whistle to stop the play or throw a yellow flag to mark the location of the foul. The offending team may then receive a penalty for breaking the rules. In most cases when a penalty occurs, the offending team is assessed a penalty of five, ten, or fifteen yards. Common offensive penalties include holding and illegal procedure, such as a false start. Common defensive penalties include pass interference and offsides, which occurs when a defensive player is across the line of scrimmage when the ball is snapped.

Time Is Ticking

Officials also keep track of the play clock and game time. The play clock is a device used to speed up the pace of play. The center must snap the ball before the play clock expires, or else the team is penalized for delaying the game. In the NFL, the play clock normally counts off forty seconds. In college games, the play clock timer is set for thirty seconds.

Game time is divided into two halves, which are divided into two periods, or quarters. In the NFL and college, teams play four fifteen-minute quarters. High schools use twelve-minute quarters. After each quarter, teams switch which end zone they are defending in order to keep the game fair. If

In addition to flags and whistles, officials use hand signals to communicate with others on the field. This head linesman (*opposite page*) indicates that it is fourth down by holding up a closed fist.

Football Lingo

Football has its own special vocabulary, or lingo. If you want to understand what the TV game announcers are talking about, it will help to know a few of these colorful terms:

bomb A long forward pass.

clip To block an opponent illegally from behind, usually at leg level.

flea flicker A trick offensive play in which the quarterback hands the ball to a running back, making the defense think it is a running play. The running back, however, tosses the ball back to the quarterback, who throws a long pass.

gridiron A football field.

hang time The amount of time a punt remains in the air.

move the chains To gain ten yards and make a first down; the "chains" is the slang term for the first-down marker.

pigskin A slang term for a football. In the nineteenth century, footballs were made from inflated pig bladders.

red zone The area between the twenty-yard line and the end zone. When a team is in the red zone, they are threatening to score.

rush To move the ball by running.

shotgun An offensive formation, used especially for passing, in which the quarterback receives the snap several yards behind the line of scrimmage.

spike The act of slamming the ball to the ground after succeeding in an important play, as after scoring a touchdown.

squib kick A kickoff in which the ball is kicked low so that it will bounce along the ground, making it difficult to field and return.

zebras Football officials, so-called because of their uniforms—black-and-white-striped shirt, white pants, black belt, and black shoes.

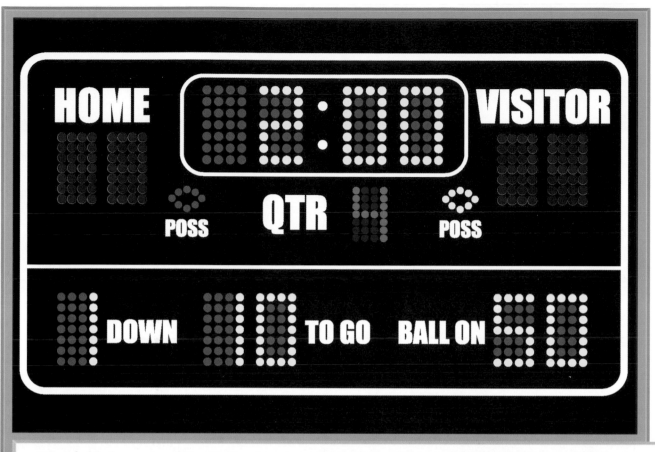

Most fields have scoreboards like this one, which shows the score, the down being played, the yards to go to get a first down, and the spot of the ball on the field. Scoreboards also show the time left on the game clock. However, the official game time is kept by the line judge, on the field.

the sun is low in the sky, or if the turf at one end of the field is torn up or muddy, one team would have a definite advantage. Switching sides ensures that field conditions do not favor one team over the other. After two quarters, the players get a short break (halftime) to drink some fluids and discuss game strategy with their coach.

CHAPTER FOUR

Getting in the Action

A rushing quarterback leaps into the end zone for a touchdown, as a diving tackler grabs only air.

Throughout the football season, kids rush out after a game to re-create the excitement of watching their favorite players perform. Many kids dream of playing football themselves and wonder how to get involved. Luckily, there are many ways to play football. Simply getting together with a group of friends from your neighborhood is one way to get started. If you don't want to tackle each other, flag football keeps all the fun without the contact. Stuff a bandana or other piece of cloth in the waistband of your pants. If someone pulls your "flag" out, then you are considered downed. Another variation is two-hand tag football. Instead of tackling, a defender must touch the ball carrier with two hands to stop the play. If you don't have access to a large, grassy field, you can even play these games on blacktop or in the street.

Joining a Team

If you are hungry for more, it may be time to get involved with an organized athletic team. Most local youth league football teams post signs when they are recruiting players for a new season. Check out the bulletin board at your local community center. Signing up usually requires a fee and the cost of your equipment.

There is no single organization that oversees all the youth football played throughout the United States, but some national groups run football teams in towns throughout the country. Pop Warner Football, for example, is a league with more than 170,000 young players in the United States. American Youth Football is a similar organization. Web sites for these organizations and others are found on pages 42–43 of this book.

Suiting Up

Once you find a team, you'll need some football equipment. Many teams include uniforms when you sign up to play. If you are just starting out, coaches will be able to tell you what you need to buy. If your team doesn't provide everything you need, there are many stores that sell football gear. Some specialty stores carry pads and any other football equipment you'll need. To better protect yourself from injuries, be picky and purchase equipment that fits correctly. If there is no specialty store near you, you can find great sporting-goods stores on the Internet that carry a wide range of supplies at reasonable prices.

In many parts of the United States, football season is also foul-weather season. If you decide to join a team, there's a good chance you will occasionally play in muddy field conditions caused by rain or snow.

Football Season

Across North America, the youth league football season usually begins in late August or early September, as the heat of summer starts to cool. You can expect to practice at least one afternoon per week during the season. Games are usually played outdoors on Saturdays.

The regular season typically lasts about three months, with the playoffs carrying the season into a fourth month. Most leagues play games in all types of weather, from blazing sun to rain to freezing temperatures, so be prepared.

Football Is for Everyone

Football is a sport not just for boys. For many years, our society worried that football was too rough for girls and tried to keep them from playing. But girls tackled the problem and found a way to play. Today, there are teams for girls at all levels, even the pros. The Women's Professional Football League has seventeen teams across the United States.

At the end of the season, the two teams with the most wins usually play against each other in a playoff to determine the champion. In bigger leagues, there may even be a couple rounds of playoff games to determine the champion.

The Next Level

Youth leagues field teams for kids from ages five to fifteen. If you're crazy about football and want to keep playing past that age, check out the activities at your school. Many high schools have their own football teams. Each year, the coaches hold tryouts to choose the members of the team. Some schools have two levels of players: Newer players make up the junior varsity squad, and the more accomplished players make up the varsity team. Many high school varsity teams enjoy heated rivalries with nearby schools.

The best players on high school football teams sometimes attract the attention of colleges and universities. These players are offered scholarships to attend classes and play football for the college.

The ultimate achievement for the football athlete is playing at the professional level. Professional football players are truly the best of the best. Only the finest college players make the jump to the NFL, CFL, or the Arena Football League. It takes complete dedication to your sport to be a professional player.

Playing football requires a strong body, so weight training is now an important part of most high school programs. Follow the advice of a coach or trainer who understands the principles of weight training. Overtraining can result in fatigue and muscle injuries.

Getting Physical

There is no question that football is a physical sport. You've probably seen crunching tackles on television. Once you're on the field, you'll find out just how that crunch feels. You must take great care of your body in order to stay healthy and enjoy the sport. Some people worry that football is too violent, but research has shown that injuries are fairly uncommon in youth football. The U.S. Consumer Product Safety Commission recently found that players in organized youth football sustained fewer injuries than other kids playing soccer, skateboarding, or bike riding. Proper equipment and coaching help prevent many injuries. Playing with other kids your own size also helps. Youth organizations like Pop Warner Football follow height and weight charts to place players at the right level.

Avoiding Injury

Football equipment and rules are designed to prevent injuries. Despite this, players do sometimes get hurt. Some injuries are the result of bad luck, but many can be prevented by being smart and using proper running and tackling techniques.

The most common injuries in football are strains, sprains, and bruises. A strain occurs when a muscle or tendon is twisted, pulled, or torn. Tendons are the cords of tissue that connect muscles to bone. A sprain is similar to a strain, but it is the stretching or tearing of a ligament instead of a tendon. Ligaments are bands of tough tissue that attach bone to bone.

Training for the Field

You can reduce the risk of injury greatly by taking care of your body—and not only on game day. Regular daily exercise is a must. Your lungs, bones, and muscles must all be strong. If you are playing football, or plan to play, fuel your body with healthful food and get plenty of exercise throughout the week. Take the time to warm up before a game by stretching your muscles and moving your joints. Also, drink plenty of fluids, especially when playing in hot weather. Take regular breaks during practice and games to replace water lost through sweat.

If you are on a football team, take your weekly practices seriously. By practicing well, you learn the plays and train your body for the full game on the weekend. Players who are serious about the sport often follow specific exercise routines. The best players are not just wrapped in muscle. They are flexible, too, and have the endurance to give their best effort for the entire game. A player in top shape can cross the field in a burst of speed without

The coach looks on as players stretch during practice. Proper warm-up exercises before games and practices greatly reduce the risk of injuries.

doubling over to catch his breath. Training and conditioning are as important as any play on the field.

Now that you've learned the football basics, you're ready to start playing the great American game. As you play more, you will find that you can always improve your game. But whether you are starring on your high school team or playing flag football in your backyard, it is important to remember that football is a game, and the most important thing is to have fun.

GLOSSARY

burly Large and sturdy.

chaos Confusion and disorder.

cleat A pointed piece of hard rubber attached to the underside of football shoes to provide traction.

endurance The physical ability to continue with a difficult, tiring task.

hash marks Yard-marking lines between the goal lines on a football field; at the beginning of each play, an official places the ball on a hash mark.

line of scrimmage A line parallel to the goal lines where football linemen line up at the start of each play.

penalty A punishment imposed on a team or competitor for breaking a game rule.

punt A football play in which the ball is dropped from the hands and kicked before it touches the ground.

recruit To enroll or seek to enroll.

revolutionary New and bringing about great change.

rivalry Competition, usually between evenly matched teams.

spectators People who view a sporting event.

FOR MORE INFORMATION

Arena Football League
105 Madison Avenue, 9th Floor
New York, NY 10016
(212) 252-8100
Web site: http://www.arenafootball.com

National Football League
280 Park Avenue
New York, NY 10017
(212) 450-2000
Web site: http://www.nfl.com

Professional Football Researchers Association
12870 Route 30, #39
North Huntingdon, PA 15642
Web site: http://www.footballresearch.com

Pro Football Hall of Fame
2121 George Halas Drive NW
Canton, OH 44708
(330) 456-8207
Web site: http://www.profootballhof.com

Girls'/Women's Football Resources

Independent Women's Football League
Web site: http://www.iwflsports.com

Women's Professional Football League
232 Belmont Street
Hurst, TX 76053
(877) WPFL-NOW (973-5669)
Web site: http://www.womensprofootball.com

Youth Football Organizations

American Youth Football & Cheer
Web site: http://www.americanyouthfootball.com
(888) 438-2816

Pop Warner Little Scholars, Inc.
586 Middletown Boulevard, Suite C-100
Langhorne, PA 19047
(215) 752-2691
Web site: http://www.popwarner.com

Web Sites

Due to the changing nature of Internet links, Rosen Publishing has developed an online list of Web sites related to the subject of this book. This site is updated regularly. Please use this link to access the list:

http://www.rosenlinks.com/scc/foot

FOR FURTHER READING

Buckley, James, Jr. *America's Greatest Game: The Real Story of Football and the National Football League*. New York, NY: Hyperion Books for Children, 1998.

Patey, R. L. *The Illustrated Rules of Football*. Nashville, TN: Hambleton-Hill Publishing, 1995.

Smith, Stewart, and Chris Johnson. *Get Fit for High School Football*. Long Island City, NY: Hatherleigh Press, 2001.

Stewart, Mark. *The Super Bowl*. New York, NY: Franklin Watts, 2002.

Tuttle, Dennis. *The Composite Guide to Football*. Philadelphia, PA: Chelsea House Publishers, 1998.

BIBLIOGRAPHY

American Academy of Orthopaedic Surgeons. "Sprains and Strains."
   Retrieved January 29, 2006 (http://www.orthoinfo.aaos.org).

Arena Football League. "AFL 101: Rules of Arena Football and the Basics of
   the Game." Retrieved January 24, 2006 (http://www.arenafootball.com/
   ViewArticle.dbml?DB_OEM_ID=3500&KEY=&ATCLID=99180).

Football.com. "Rules and Information." Retrieved January 23, 2006
   (http://www.football.com/rulesabc/play_game.shtml).

Hannon, Kent. "Is Football Safe for Kids?" Retrieved January 10, 2006
   (http://www.metroyouthfootball.com/sports_illustrated.htm).

National Institute of Arthritis and Musculoskeletal and Skin Diseases.
   "Childhood Sports Injuries and Their Prevention: A Guide for Parents
   with Ideas for Kids." Retrieved February 10, 2006 (http://www.
   niams.nih.gov).

Oldham, Scott. "Bombs Away." *Popular Mechanics*, October 16, 2001.
   Retrieved March 13, 2006 (http://www.popularmechanics.com/
   science/sports/1283226.html?page=1&c=y).

Professional Football Researchers Association. "Dribble, Hack, and Split:
   The Origins of Soccer and Rugby." Retrieved January 23, 2006 (http://
   www.footballresearch.com/articles/frpage.cfm?topic=b-to1800).

Stewart, Mark. *Football: A History of the Gridiron Game*. New York, NY:
   Franklin Watts, 1998.

INDEX

About the Author

Brian Wingate has been an avid follower of the National Football League for twenty years. He developed a love for the game playing youth football throughout his childhood. An experienced writer in the field of youth sports, Wingate has published books covering soccer, skateboarding, and BMX racing, in addition to football. He lives in Tennessee with his wife and children.

Photo Credits

Cover (left, right, group, and field), pp. 1, 13, 14, 15, 19, 29, 30, 36 © Shutterstock; p. 3 (ball) © istockphoto.com/Buz Zoller; p. 3 (helmet) © istockphoto.com/Stefan Klein; p. 4 © Mary Evans Picture Library/The Image Works; p. 6 Library of Congress Prints and Photographs Division; p. 7 © Getty Images; p. 10 © Darryl Bautista; pp. 12, 16 © Caleb Simpson/Icon SMI; pp. 17, 18, 22, 27 © John Green/Icon SMI; p. 20 © Mike Carlson/Icon SMI; p. 24 © istockphoto.com/Doug Webb; p. 26 © istockphoto.com/Matt Matthews; p. 33 © istockphoto.com/Elianet Ortiz; p. 34 © istockphoto.com/Kirk Strickland; p. 38 © istockphoto.com/Pavel Losevsky; p. 40 © istockphoto.com/Eliza Snow; back cover (soccer ball) © www.istockphoto.com/Pekka Jaakkola; back cover (paintball gear) © www.istockphoto.com/Jason Maehl; back cover (football helmet) © www.istockphoto.com/Stefan Klein; back cover (football) © www.istockphoto.com/Buz Zoller; back cover (baseball gear) © www.istockphoto.com/Charles Silvey; back cover (basketball) © www.istockphoto.com/Dusty Cline.

Designer: Nelson Sá; **Editor:** Christopher Roberts
Photo Researcher: Jeffrey Wendt